We Like Fishing

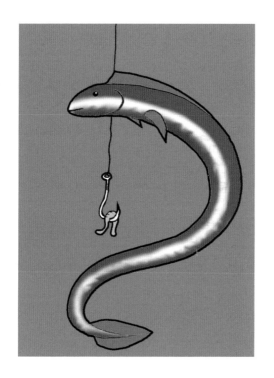

written by Pam Holden
illustrated by Samer Hatam

1

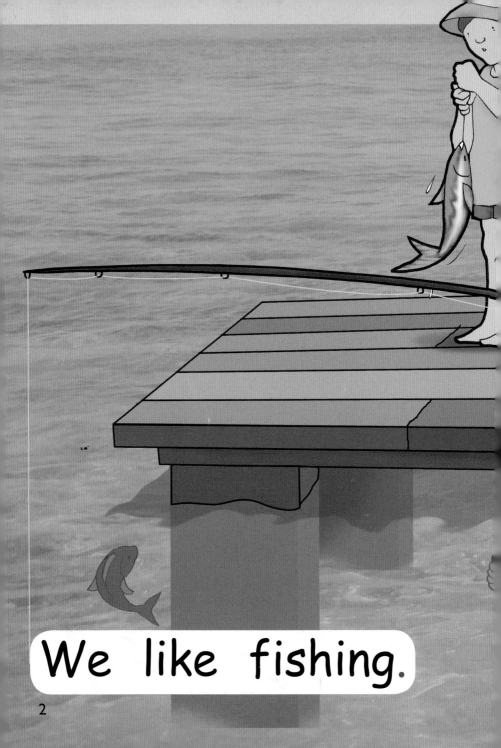

We like fishing.

We like fishing in the lake.

We like fishing
in the boat.

We like fishing
in the waves.

We like fishing
in the stream.

We like fishing
in the river.

We like fishing
in the pools.

We like fishing
in the sea!

The	we
in	like
We	the

Emergent Level
Fiction Set C

GUIDED READING	R/R INTERVENTION	DRA LEVEL
B	2	1-2

F&P Text Level Gradient™
Officially Leveled by **Fountas & Pinnell**

Red Rocket™ Readers

Engineered by
Flying Start Books

www.redrocketreaders.com

ISBN 978-1-927197-52-3

9 781927 197523